LITTLE TIGER PRESS
An imprint of Magi Publications
1 The Coda Centre, 189 Munster Road, London SW6 6AW
www.littletigerpress.com

First published in Great Britain 2006
This edition published 2006

Text and illustrations copyright © Catherine Rayner 2006
Catherine Rayner has asserted her right to be identified as the author and illustrator
of this work under the Copyright, Designs and Patents Act, 1988

Printed in Belgium
4 6 8 10 9 7 5 3

Thank you, Mum, Dad, Brian and Colin ~ C R

AUGUSTUS AND HIS
SMILE

CATHERINE RAYNER

LITTLE TIGER PRESS
London

Augustus the tiger was sad.

He had lost his smile.

So he did a HUGE tigery stretch

and set off to find it.

First he crept
under a cluster
of bushes. He found
a small, shiny beetle,
but he couldn't see
his smile.

Then he climbed to the tops of the tallest trees.
He found birds that chirped and called,
but he couldn't find his smile.

Further and further Augustus searched.

He scaled the crests of the highest mountains where the snow clouds swirled, making frost patterns in the freezing air.

He swam to the bottom of the deepest oceans
and splished and splashed with shoals of tiny, shiny fish.

He pranced and paraded through the
largest desert, making shadow shapes
in the sun. Augustus padded further

and further

through shifting sand

until . . .

. . . pitter
patter
pitter
patter

drip

drop

plop!

Augustus danced
and raced
as raindrops bounced
and flew.

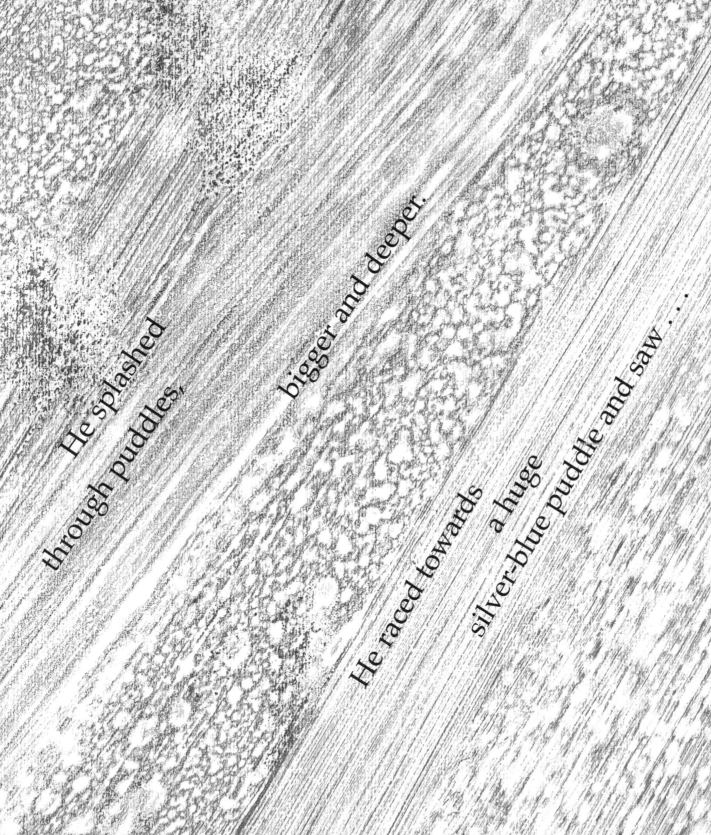

He splashed
through puddles,

bigger and deeper.

He raced towards
a huge
silver-blue puddle and saw . . . .

. . . there, under his nose

. . . his smile!

And Augustus realised that his smile would be there,
whenever he was happy.

He only had to swim with the fish
or dance in the puddles,
or climb the mountains and look at the world –
for happiness was everywhere around him.

Augustus was so pleased that
he hopped

and skipped . . .

. . . and jumped away,
smiling.

Amazing tiger facts

Augustus is a Siberian tiger.

Siberian tigers are the biggest cats in the world!
They live in Southern Russia and Northern China where
the winters are very cold.

Most tigers are orange with black stripes. The stripes
make them hard to see when they walk through tall
weeds and grasses.

Tigers are good swimmers and like to cool down by
sitting in waterholes.

Every tiger has a different pattern of stripes – like a
human fingerprint.

Tigers are in danger . . .

Tigers are only hunted by one animal . . . HUMANS!
And humans are ruining the land where tigers live.

There are more tigers living in zoos and nature reserves
than in the wild. There are only about 6,000 tigers left in
the wild.

Help save the tiger!

World Wildlife Fund (WWF)
Panda House
Weyside Park
Godalming
Surrey GU7 1XR
Tel: 01483 426 444
Website: www.wwf.org.uk

David Shepherd Wildlife Foundation
61 Smithbrook Kilns
Cranleigh
Surrey GU6 8JJ
Tel: 01483 272 323/267 924
Website: www.davidshepherd.org

For information regarding any other Little Tiger Press titles or for our catalogue, please contact us:

Little Tiger Press, 1 The Coda Centre, 189 Munster Road, London SW6 6AW

Tel: 020 7385 6333 • Fax: 020 7385 7333 • E-mail: info@littletiger.co.uk • Website: www.littletigerpress.com